Leaping Lizards

Mary Elizabeth Salzmann
Illustrated by Neena Chawla

Consulting Editor, Diane Craig, M.A./Reading Specialist

ABDO
Publishing Company

Published by ABDO Publishing Company, 4940 Viking Drive, Edina, Minnesota 55435.

Printed in the United States.

Credits
Edited by: Pam Price
Curriculum Coordinator: Nancy Tuminelly
Cover and Interior Design and Production: Mighty Media
Photo Credits: James Gerholdt/Peter Arnold Inc., Corbis Images, Corel, Photodisc, ShutterStock

Library of Congress Cataloging-in-Publication Data

Salzmann, Mary Elizabeth, 1968-
    Leaping lizards / Mary Elizabeth Salzmann; illustrated by Neena Chawla.
       p. cm. -- (Fact & fiction. Critter chronicles)
    Summary: Lizzie Lizard is so excited about trying out her birthday present--a trampoline--that she forgets the most important safety rule. Alternating pages provide facts about lizards.
    ISBN 10 1-59928-450-2 (hardcover)
    ISBN 10 1-59928-451-0 (paperback)

    ISBN 13 978-1-59928-450-7 (hardcover)
    ISBN 13 978-1-59928-451-4 (paperback)
    [1. Birthdays--Fiction. 2. Trampoline--Fiction. 3. Parties--Fiction. 4. Lizards--Fiction] I. Chawla, Neena, ill.
II. Title. III. Series.

    PZ7.S15565Lea 2006
    [E]--dc22

                                                                                    2006005544

SandCastle Level: Fluent

SandCastle™ books are created by a professional team of educators, reading specialists, and content developers around five essential components—phonemic awareness, phonics, vocabulary, text comprehension, and fluency—to assist young readers as they develop reading skills and strategies and increase their general knowledge. All books are written, reviewed, and leveled for guided reading, early reading intervention, and Accelerated Reader® programs for use in shared, guided, and independent reading and writing activities to support a balanced approach to literacy instruction. The SandCastle™ series has four levels that correspond to early literacy development. The levels help teachers and parents select appropriate books for young readers.

| **Emerging Readers** | **Beginning Readers** | **Transitional Readers** | **Fluent Readers** |
| (no flags) | (1 flag) | (2 flags) | (3 flags) |

These levels are meant only as a guide. All levels are subject to change.

FACT & FICTION

This series provides early fluent readers the opportunity to develop reading comprehension strategies and increase fluency. These books are appropriate for guided, shared, and independent reading.

FACT The left-hand pages incorporate realistic photographs to enhance readers' understanding of informational text.

FICTION The right-hand pages engage readers with an entertaining, narrative story that is supported by whimsical illustrations.

The Fact and Fiction pages can be read separately to improve comprehension through questioning, predicting, making inferences, and summarizing. They can also be read side-by-side, in spreads, which encourages students to explore and examine different writing styles.

FACT OR FICTION? This fun quiz helps reinforce students' understanding of what is real and not real.

SPEED READ The text-only version of each section includes word-count rulers for fluency practice and assessment.

GLOSSARY Higher-level vocabulary and concepts are defined in the glossary.

SandCastle™ would like to hear from you.

Tell us your stories about reading this book. What was your favorite page? Was there something hard that you needed help with? Share the ups and downs of learning to read. To get posted on the ABDO Publishing Company Web site, send us an e-mail at:

sandcastle@abdopublishing.com

Most lizards eat insects, worms, or rodents. Some eat only plants, while others eat plants and animals.

Today is Lizzie Lizard's birthday!
Her mother makes Lizzie her favorite
breakfast, oatmeal, bacon, and orange juice.

Lizards are reptiles. Because they are cold-blooded, they bask in the sun to warm up and find shady spots when they need to cool off.

After breakfast, Lizzie opens presents from her parents. She gets an electric blanket to keep her warm at night and a new yellow outfit. "I'll wear it to my party this afternoon," she says. "Thank you for the presents, Mama and Papa!"

Baby lizards are born knowing how to feed and take care of themselves, so their parents don't have to.

"Wait, Honey," her father says. "There is one more. Look outside."

Lizzie looks out the window and squeals, "A trampoline! Oh thank you! It's going to be so much fun!"

"Just remember the rules," her mother says. "Always close the safety net and either your father or I must be present."

9

Lizards' scales are colored to blend in to their surroundings. Some lizards change color as they move around or when they are hurt or afraid.

"Okay," Lizzie agrees. She dresses in her new outfit and runs outside to try out the trampoline. "Whee," she shouts as she jumps and bounces.

Lizards have good eyesight and move
quickly, so they can escape predators and
catch prey.

Suddenly Lizzie realizes that she forgot to close the net and is about to go flying off! Her father sees what is happening, darts over to the trampoline, and catches Lizzie before she falls. "Lizzie! What did we tell you about closing the net," he scolds.

Fiction

Lizards' life spans range from a few years to over 50 years. Large lizards tend to live longer than small lizards.

"I'm sorry, Papa," Lizzie sniffs. "That was scary. I won't forget to close the net again!" She climbs back onto the trampoline, carefully closes the net, and practices until it's time for her birthday party.

15

If a lizard is grabbed by its tail, the tail may come off and keep wiggling. This distracts the predator while the lizard escapes. The tail grows back but looks different.

The first guests to arrive are Lizzie's best friends, Gertie Gecko and Katie Chameleon. "Katie! Gertie! Look at my new trampoline," Lizzie exclaims, bouncing on her tail.

"Wow! It looks like fun," Gertie says.

"May I try it?" Katie asks.

"Sure," Lizzie replies.

17

There are over 4,000 different species of lizards, including chameleons, geckos, iguanas, and skinks.

Pretty soon, everyone is there. They eat birthday cake and take turns on the trampoline. Lizzie declares, "Look at us! We're leaping lizards!"

FACT OR FiCTiON?

Read each statement below. Then decide whether it's from the FACT section or the FiCTiON section!

  1. Lizards are cold-blooded.

  2. Lizards like to jump on trampolines.

  3. A lizard's tail may break off if it is grabbed.

  4. Lizards have birthday parties.

ANSWERS
1. fact 2. fiction 3. fact 4. fiction

Most lizards eat insects, worms, or rodents. Some 8
eat only plants, while others eat plants and animals. 17

Lizards are reptiles. Because they are cold-blooded, 25
they bask in the sun to warm up and find shady spots 37
when they need to cool off. 43

Baby lizards are born knowing how to feed and take 53
care of themselves, so their parents don't have to. 62

Lizards' scales are colored to blend in to their 71
surroundings. Some lizards change color as they move 79
around or when they are hurt or afraid. 87

Lizards have good eyesight and move quickly, so 95
they can escape predators and catch prey. 102

Lizards' life spans range from a few years to over 50 113
years. Large lizards tend to live longer than small lizards. 123

If a lizard is grabbed by its tail, the tail may come off 136
and keep wiggling. This distracts the predator while the 145
lizard escapes. The tail grows back but looks different. 154

There are over 4,000 different species of lizards, 162
including chameleons, geckos, iguanas, and skinks. 168

21

Today is Lizzie Lizard's birthday! Her mother 7
makes Lizzie her favorite breakfast, oatmeal, 13
bacon, and orange juice. 17

After breakfast, Lizzie opens presents from her 24
parents. She gets an electric blanket to keep her 33
warm at night and a new yellow outfit. "I'll wear 43
it to my party this afternoon," she says. "Thank 52
you for the presents, Mama and Papa!" 59

"Wait, Honey," her father says. "There is one 67
more. Look outside." 70

Lizzie looks out the window and squeals, "A 78
trampoline! Oh thank you! It's going to be so 87
much fun!" 89

"Just remember the rules," her mother says. 96
"Always close the safety net and either your father 105
or I must be present." 110

"Okay," Lizzie agrees. She dresses in her new 118
outfit and runs outside to try out the trampoline. 127
"Whee," she shouts as she jumps and bounces. 135

22

Suddenly Lizzie realizes that she forgot to close the net and is about to go flying off! Her father sees what is happening, darts over to the trampoline, and catches Lizzie before she falls. "Lizzie! What did we tell you about closing the net," he scolds.

"I'm sorry, Papa," Lizzie sniffs. "That was scary. I won't forget to close the net again!" She climbs back onto the trampoline, carefully closes the net, and practices until it's time for her birthday party.

The first guests to arrive are Lizzie's best friends, Gertie Gecko and Katie Chameleon. "Katie! Gertie! Look at my new trampoline," Lizzie exclaims, bouncing on her tail.

"Wow! It looks like fun," Gertie says.

"May I try it?" Katie asks.

"Sure," Lizzie replies.

Pretty soon, everyone is there. They eat birthday cake and take turns on the trampoline. Lizzie declares, "Look at us! We're leaping lizards!"

GLOSSARY

bask. to enjoy lying or sitting in the sun

distract. to cause to turn away from one's original focus of interest

predator. an animal that hunts others

prey. an animal that is hunted or caught for food

rodent. a mammal with large, sharp front teeth, such as a rat, mouse, or squirrel

scale. one of the small, hard pieces of skin that cover the bodies of fish, reptiles, and some mammals

species. a group of related beings

surroundings. the conditions and things around someone or something

To see a complete list of SandCastle™ books and other nonfiction titles from ABDO Publishing Company, visit www.abdopublishing.com or contact us at: 4940 Viking Drive, Edina, Minnesota 55435 • 1-800-800-1312 • fax: 1-952-831-1632